LITTLE MISS STAR

by Roger Hargreaves

D1355525

EGMONT

Little Miss Star lived in Twinkle Cottage.

Now.

I'll tell you a secret.

You promise not to tell anyone else.

Don't you?

All her life, Little Miss Star had dreamed
of being famous.

She desperately wanted to be famous so that everyone
would recognise her and ask her for her autograph,
and she would have her photograph in all the papers.

But, she didn't know how.

She dreamed about it when she went to bed at night, and she dreamed about it when she woke up in the morning.

But, how could she become famous?

She had no idea!

Twinkle Cottage was just outside Tiddlyville, which is a small town a long way from where you live.

And even further from where I live!

One morning, Little Miss Star was out shopping in Tiddlyville.

"Hello, Miss Star," everybody called out to her as she walked down the street.

She was very popular.

But she wasn't famous!

And she wanted to be.

But, it was on that very same morning that
Little Miss Star had an idea.

An idea?

Not likely!

The Idea!

She was walking past one of the shops in Tiddlyville when something caught her eye.

She stopped.

And stared!

You see, it was that something that was to make her fame and fortune.

Would you like to know what it was?

I'll tell you later!

She jumped for joy.

And hugged herself with glee.

And she hurried home to Twinkle Cottage as fast as ever her little legs would carry her.

She was going to be famous!

She knew it!

She ran upstairs and hastily packed a suitcase.

Then she hurried downstairs, locked the front door of Twinkle Cottage, and went to the bus stop.

The bus came, and she hopped onto it.

"Fares, please," said the driver.

"I want to go to Tiddlyport Airville," said Little Miss Star excitedly.

The driver scratched his head.

"You don't by any chance mean Tiddlyville Airport?" he asked.

Little Miss Star nodded, and blushed.

The driver smiled, and gave her a ticket.

At the airport Little Miss Star bought an airline ticket.

Where to?

I'll tell you later!

She had never been on an airliner before.

It was all very exciting!

"Hello," said an air hostess. "What's your name?"

"Little Miss Star," she said.

"And where are you going?" asked the hostess.

"I'm going," said Little Miss Star, "to be famous!"

"Oh," said the hostess.

After the airliner had landed, Little Miss Star collected her suitcase, and took a taxi!

Where to?

I'll tell you now!

To a house!

The taxi drove up, and Little Miss Star got out.

She knocked on the door.

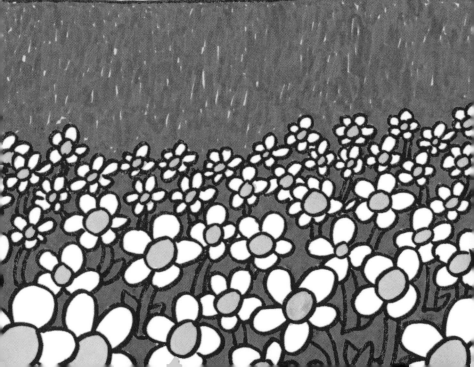

She could hear footsteps coming to the door, and then the door opened.

There, before her, stood a large man.

"Hello," he grinned. "Who are you?"

"I'm Little Miss Star and I want to be famous!" she said, all in a rush.

"Oh, you do, do you?" laughed the man.

"Well, you'd better come in, and I'll see what I can do to help."

Three weeks later Little Miss Star, home again in Twinkle Cottage, just couldn't sleep for excitement.

"Tomorrow is the day," she thought to herself.

"Tomorrow I'll be famous!"

But she did get to sleep eventually, with a beautiful smile all over her face.

The early morning sun, streaming in through the bedroom window of Twinkle Cottage, woke her.

She jumped out of bed.

Little Miss Star was much too excited to eat breakfast.

She hurried into Tiddlyville.

She rushed up to one of the shops.

Which shop?

I'll tell you later!

The window blind of the shop was drawn.

So she waited.

And she waited.

And she waited some more!

But then, at nine o'clock on the dot, the window blind was raised and there, in the window, oh bliss!

She jumped for joy.

"I'm famous," she gasped.

And, do you know what was there, filling the whole of the window?

I'll tell you now!

Hundreds of books!

And, on the front cover of every book, there she was!

And there! At the top! In big bold letters, it said:

**LITTLE MISS
STAR**

"Oh me!" she gasped.

And there! Underneath! In colour, was a picture of herself!

"Oh my!" she gasped.

And there, inside, was her story!

LITTLE MISS STAR

by Roger Hargreaves

And here!

You are!

Reading it!